Tim's GOODBYE

Written and illustrated by
Steven Salerno

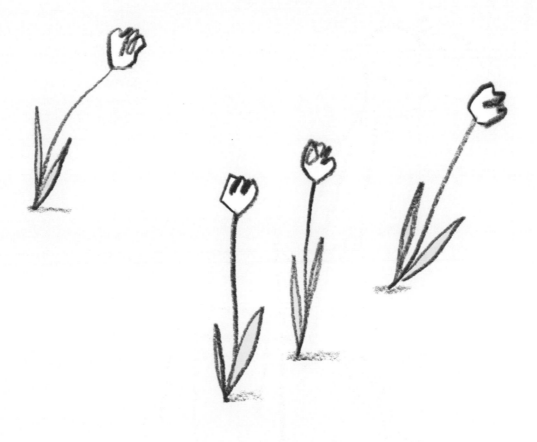

FARRAR STRAUS GIROUX
New York

On this sunny day Margot was feeling sad.

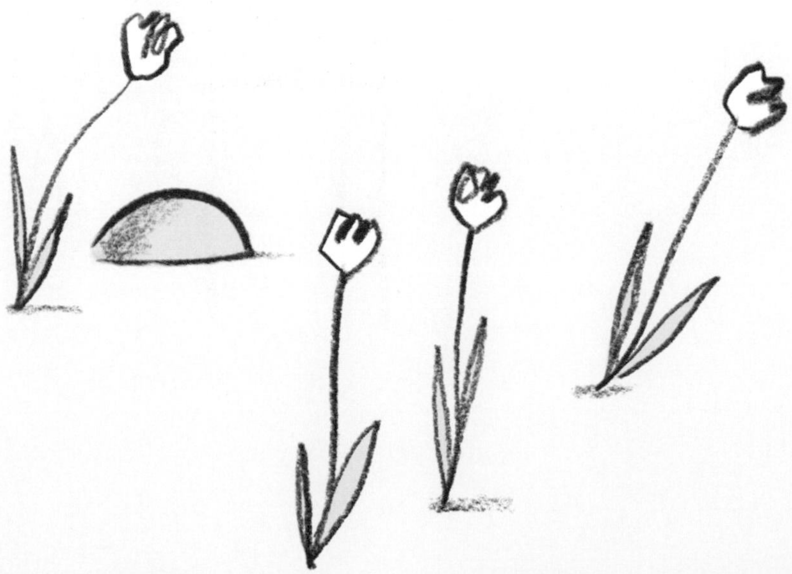

Tim was gone.

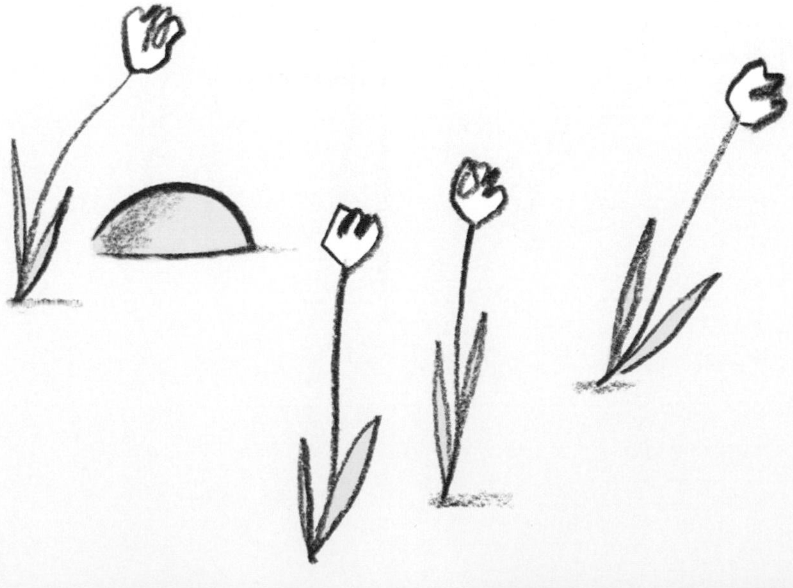

She wiped away her tears and left.

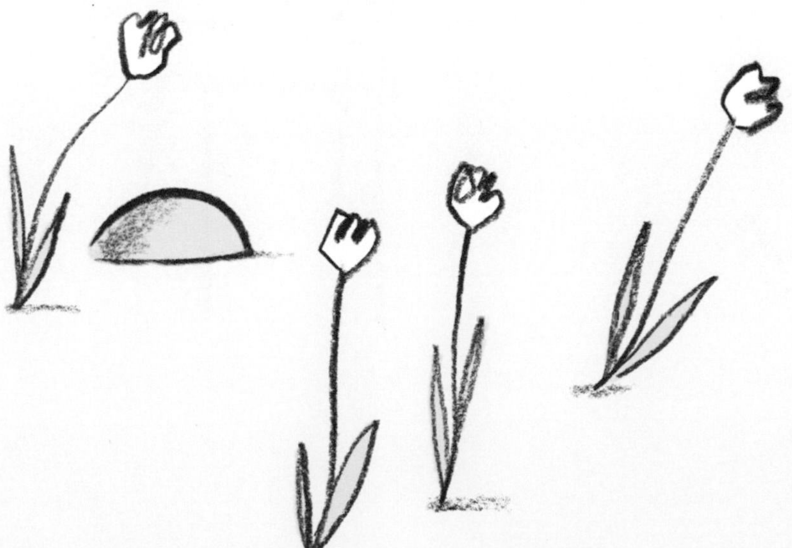

Roger suddenly appeared,

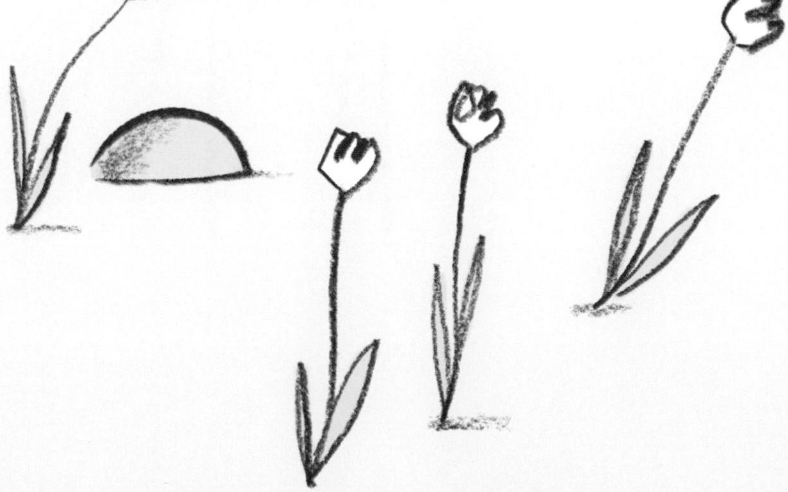

followed by Vincent.

They departed together.

. . . and Margot returned.

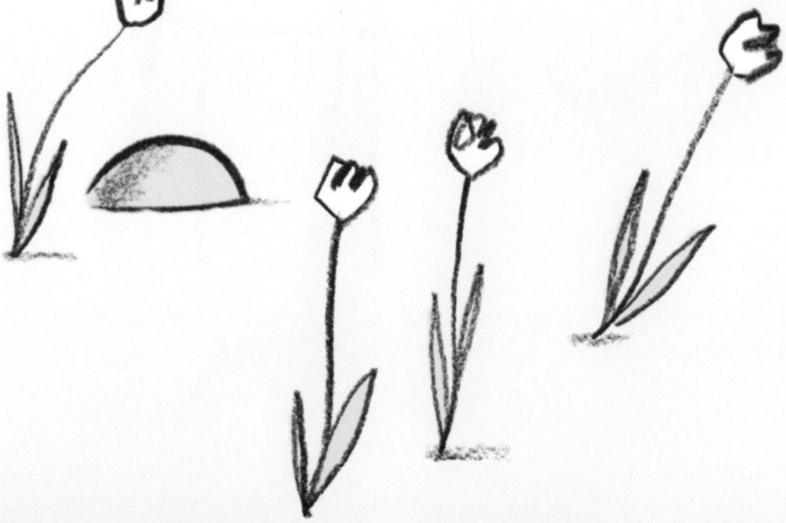

Buddy jumped in . . .

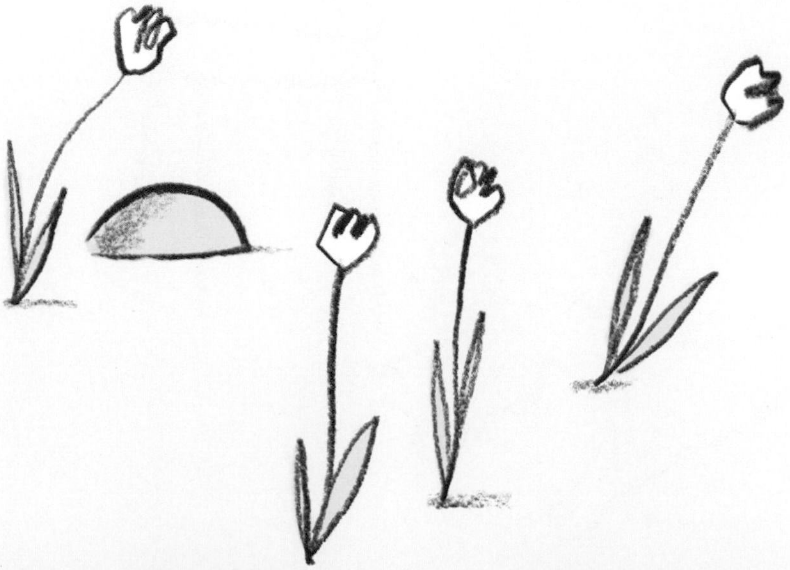

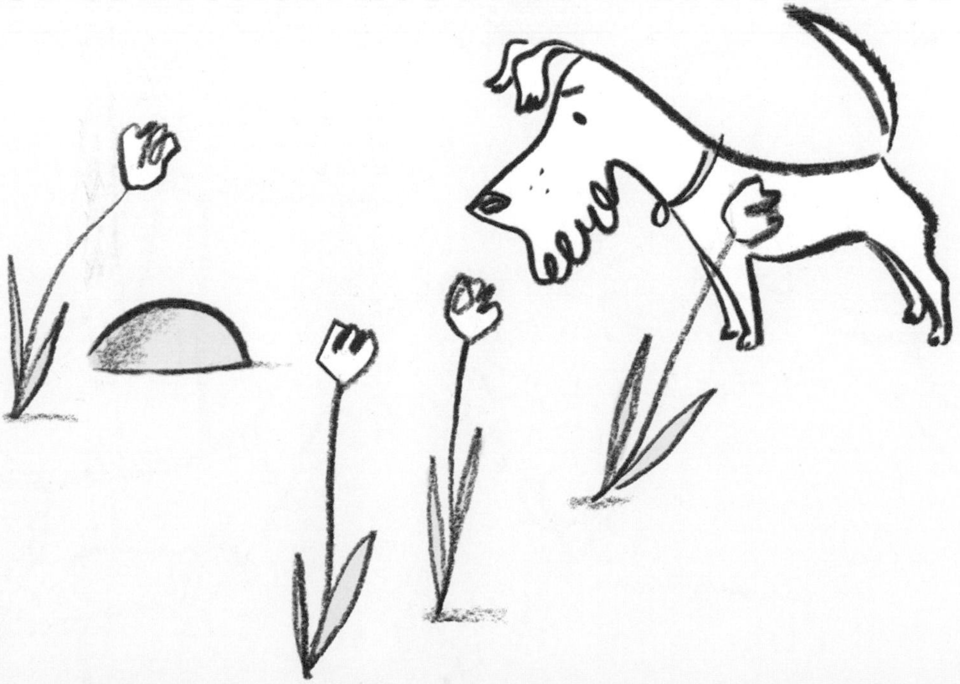

Melinda arrived, carrying her French horn.

So did Otto, wearing his best hat.

Roger and Vincent came back with an empty box.

They all gathered around . . .

. . . as Margot gently lifted Tim
and placed him into the empty box.

Otto covered Tim with flowers.

Roger tied the balloons and
Melinda played a cheerful melody.

Margot waved a final goodbye to her turtle.

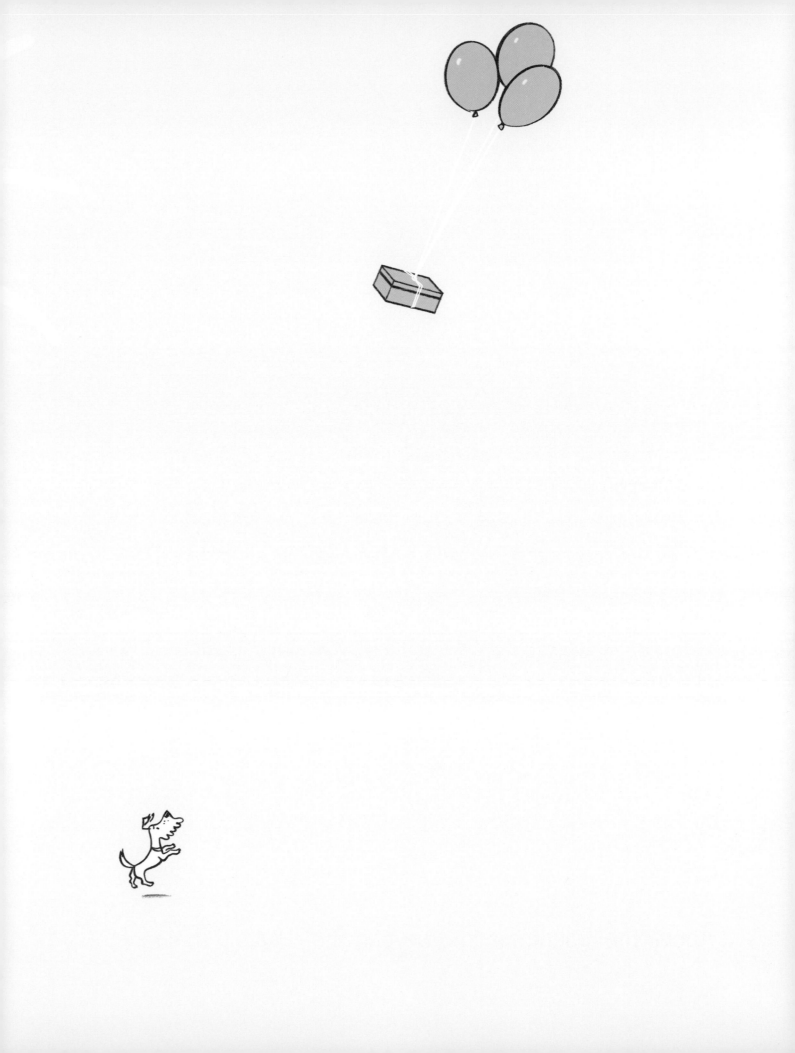

Above the mountains and beyond the clouds Tim soared . . .

. . . to a place where he basked in the warm sun and swam in cool waters, forever a happy turtle.

Margot gazed up at the stars for a long time . . .

. . . and didn't feel sad anymore.